Beetles

Rose Inserra

Contents

What Are Beetles?

Beetles are winged insects.
They are the largest group of animals in the world.
There are over 350 000 kinds of beetles.

Beetles can be different sizes.
Tiny beetles are smaller than a dot, and large beetles can be up to 17 centimetres long.

Beetles are found all over the world, except in Antarctica.
They live in many different places – in gardens, above and below the dirt, in rubbish, and even in buildings.

ladybird

darkling beetle
stag beetle
rhinoceros beetle

A beetle has three main body parts: the head, the thorax and the abdomen.

Most beetles can fly. They have four wings – two hard and two soft. The hard wings protect their bodies. The soft wings are for flying.

Some beetles have sharp mouthparts that move like teeth. They use their jaws to grasp, crush or cut food.

Beetles have **antennae** (say: *an-ten-ee*) at the top of their heads. They can smell and feel where they are with their antennae.

The first beetles lived hundreds of millions of years ago.

Parts of a Darkling Beetle

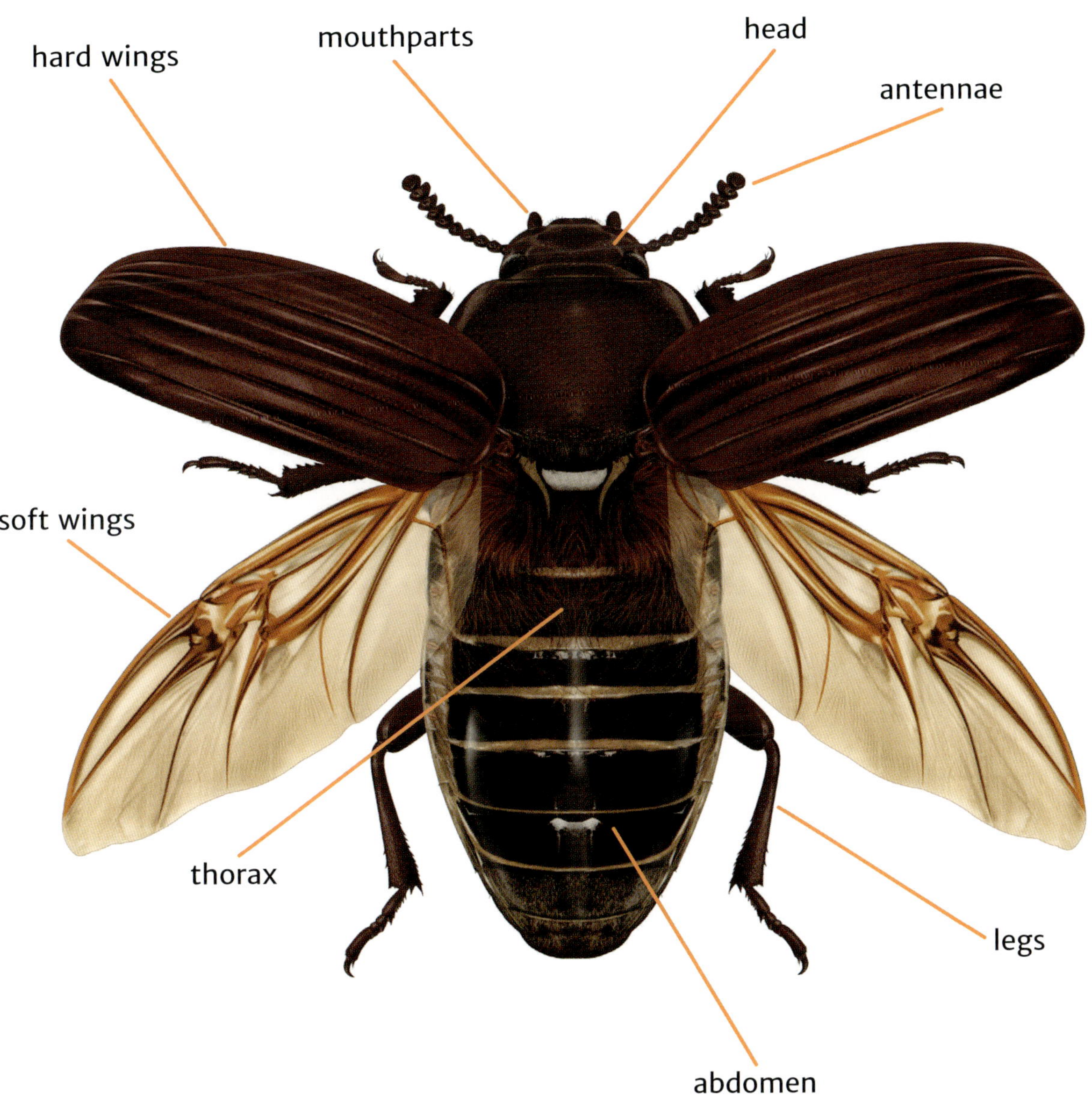

Some beetles need other insects and plants for food or shelter.

Ladybirds lay their eggs among another group of insects, called aphids (say: *ay-fids*). When the ladybirds' eggs hatch, tiny grubs called larvae (say: *lar-vee*) come out and begin to feed on the aphids.

A ladybird larva eats the tiny green aphids on a plant.

The larvae of stag beetles live underground. They feed on leaf litter and rotting dead wood, like tree stumps and roots. They need to eat a lot of food to grow.

Darkling beetles are sometimes found under rocks and in leaf litter. Some dig into wood. Others make homes in ant nests. They eat rotting plants and dead animals. They also eat living plants, fruit and grains.

The Life Cycle of a Beetle

The life cycle of a beetle has four **stages**: egg, larva, pupa and adult.

Ladybirds lay up to 40 eggs. The eggs hatch after four to ten days. Larvae come out of the eggs.

Then, a larva makes a hard case around its body, called a pupa (say: *pyoo-pa*). Inside the pupa, the larva changes into an adult ladybird.

After about two weeks, an adult ladybird comes out of the pupa.

Ladybirds are also called ladybugs and ladybeetles.

The Life Cycle of a Ladybird

Different Kinds of Beetles

Dung Beetle

Dung beetles live on piles of **dung**, or waste, from plant-eating animals like sheep, cattle, horses and elephants.

Dung beetles use their mouthparts to suck wet food from the waste.

Some dung beetles roll dung into balls.
The beetles that do this are called “rollers”.
This is because they roll the dung balls away from the piles of dung. They lay their eggs inside the dung balls.
The larvae eat the dung when they hatch.

This dung beetle is rolling dung into a ball.

Diving Beetle

Diving beetles can be found in ponds, lakes, creeks and streams.

A diving beetle has a flat, oval body. This helps it to move easily in the water.

Diving beetles are meat eaters.
They eat bugs and other insects that live in, or fall into, the water.
They also eat tadpoles and small fish.

The diving beetle's flat body helps it to glide through the water.

Predators, such as birds, fish, frogs and water spiders, like to eat diving beetles.

A water bird finds a diving beetle to eat.

Rhinoceros Beetle

Rhinoceros beetles are plant eaters.
Their larvae eat rotting plants.
The adults feed on fruit, **nectar** and tree **sap**.

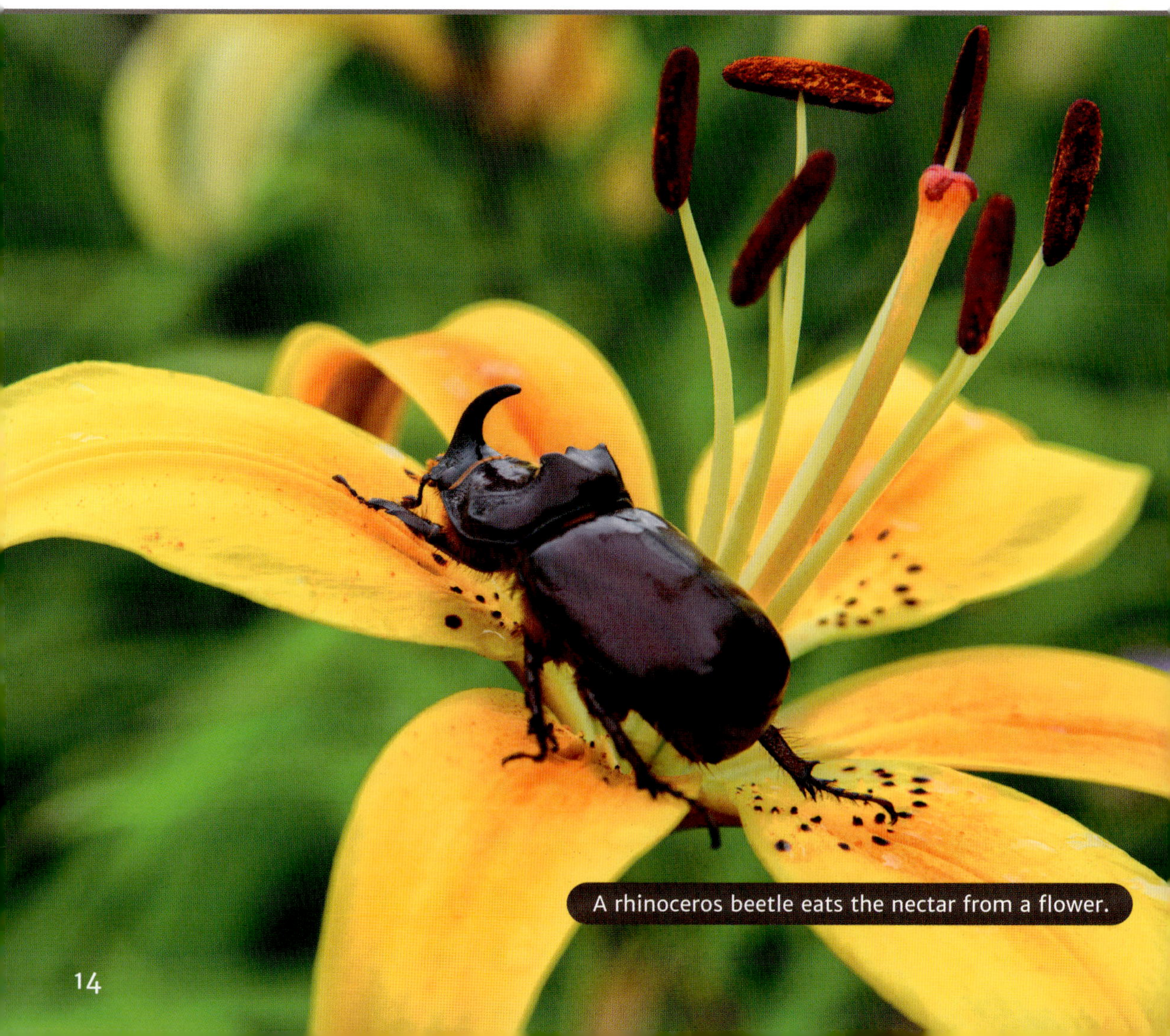

A rhinoceros beetle eats the nectar from a flower.

Male rhinoceros beetles have a long horn on their head, just like a rhinoceros.
They use it to fight with other male rhinoceros beetles.
They also have smaller horns on the sides of their head.

Two male rhinoceros beetles use their horns to fight each other.

> The rhinoceros beetle is one of the largest and strongest beetles in the world.

Firefly

Fireflies live in warm and wet places.

Most fireflies make light from a special part of their body, found under their abdomen.
The light glows during **twilight**.

Firefly light can be yellow, green or orange.
The light is sometimes a warning to predators that the firefly is not good to eat.

In the dark, fireflies look like lots of tiny lights.

Adult fireflies usually drink nectar and eat **pollen**.

Firefly larvae are meat eaters and are often seen eating snails.

A firefly larva eats a snail.

Beetles and the Environment

Beetles do important jobs.
Some beetles help farmers' crops to grow.
They feed on other insects before these pests can harm the crops.

Other beetles help to move the waste from farm animals around the fields on farms.
The animal waste helps the crops in the soil to grow.

This ladybird is eating the green aphids that are destroying an apple tree.

But some beetles are pests.
Weevils **bore** holes into plants and grains, where they lay their eggs.
They destroy dry foods like flour and rice inside people's houses.

Weevils destroy grains inside a person's home.

Beetles are important for the environment.

Some beetles provide food for animals and other insects. Other beetles help to recycle dead wood and leaf litter by feeding on it. The **nutrients** from their waste then goes back into the soil.

A beetle is a meal for this bird.

A stag beetle eats the wood of a dying tree.

Beetles are interesting insects to look at. They can be many different colours and sizes.

Some beetles are pests, but most help to keep the environment clean and healthy.

Christmas beetle

soldier beetle

Glossary

antennae (*noun*) feelers or stalks on an insect's head

bore (*verb*) to make a hole by digging or drilling

dung (*noun*) solid waste from animals

nectar (*noun*) a sweet liquid made by flowers

nutrients (*noun*) fats, vitamins, proteins and other things found in food and soil that help a plant or animal live and grow

pollen (*noun*) the powder that is found inside flowers, which helps to make new seeds

sap (*noun*) the sticky liquid inside trees and plants

stages (*noun*) the separate parts of a process

twilight (*noun*) low light just before sunrise or just after sunset

Index